Zoe's Rescue Zoo

Zoe peeped inside the crate. She could just make out a fluffy black and white bundle. The bundle wriggled – and Zoe grinned in delight. There were *two* adorable creatures, cuddled up asleep together!

Look out for:

The *Lonely Lion Cub*

The *Puzzled Penguin*

The *Silky Seal Pup*

Zoe's Rescue ZOO

The Playful Panda

Amelia Cobb

Illustrated by **Sophy Williams**

nosy crow

With special thanks to Natalie Doherty

For Nic, Steph, Joe, Iain and Frankie x

First published in the UK in 2013 by Nosy Crow Ltd
The Crow's Nest, 10a Lant St
London, SE1 1QR, UK

Nosy Crow and associated logos are trademarks and/or
registered trademarks of Nosy Crow Ltd

Text copyright © Hothouse Fiction, 2013
Illustrations © Sophy Williams, 2013

The right of Hothouse Fiction and Sophy Williams to be identified as the author
and illustrator respectively of this work has been asserted by them in accordance
with the Copyright, Designs and Patents Act 1988.

A CIP catalogue record for this book will be available from the British Library

Printed and bound in the UK by Clays Ltd, St Ives Plc

Papers used by Nosy Crow are made from wood grown in sustainable forests.

ISBN: 978 0 85763 216 6

www.nosycrow.com

Chapter One

A Treat for Daisy

Zoe Parker grinned as she raced down the path. It was Saturday morning at the Rescue Zoo and Zoe was on her way to visit some of her favourite animals. Halfway down the path she stopped at a wooden gate and reached for the pretty silver paw-print charm on her necklace.

This was no ordinary necklace – it

opened the door to every single enclosure
in the Rescue Zoo! It had been a present
from her Great-Uncle Horace, who had
built the zoo, and Zoe never took it off.
She held the charm against a small panel
on the gate and with a quiet click it
swung open.

Zoe walked into a warm, wide plain,
covered in tall grass and lush trees. Just
beyond the gate was the house where
the giraffes slept, a tall red-brick building
with a high arched doorway. Zoe shaded
her eyes from the sunshine and saw the
herd gathered at the other end of the
enclosure, drinking from a sparkling
stream. By the gate stood a wheelbarrow
full of fresh straw, and a large garden fork.
The giraffe keeper, Frankie, had promised
Zoe she could help out this morning, and

everything she needed was ready for her!

Zoe grabbed the wheelbarrow and pushed it into the giraffe house. She picked up the fork and began lifting the straw out, spreading it carefully on the ground so that the giraffes would have clean, comfortable bedding that night.

She hummed happily as she worked, enjoying the warm breeze and wondering where her best friend had got to. He had dashed off along the path in front of her that morning, too excited to slow down!

Suddenly the straw in the wheelbarrow started to wriggle. Zoe watched curiously as it shook from side to side. Then a furry little head popped out and a pair of huge, golden eyes blinked cheekily at her.

"Meep!" laughed Zoe. "There you are, you naughty thing!"

With a cheerful chirp, the tiny creature

sprang out of the wheelbarrow and climbed up on to Zoe's shoulder, sending bits of straw everywhere. Meep was a grey mouse lemur. He was very small with a long, curling tail and soft, delicate ears that stuck up in the air. He'd come to the zoo when he was just a baby, and lived with Zoe and her mum in their cottage.

"I wondered where you'd disappeared to, Meep. You're supposed to be helping me tidy the giraffe enclosure, not making a mess!" Zoe shook her head but couldn't help smiling. The little lemur was so cute that she could never *really* tell him off.

As she finished spreading out the straw, Zoe heard a gentle bray behind her and turned around. The youngest member of the giraffe herd, Daisy, had come over to greet them. She was just a few months old but she was still more than twice as tall as Zoe!

"Morning, Daisy!" called Zoe. The graceful giraffe trotted over and Zoe put down her fork and reached up to stroke her long, slender neck. Every giraffe had a different pattern of special markings that helped Zoe tell them apart. She knew this was Daisy from the pretty star shape on her forehead.

"Wow, Mum! Look!" cried an excited voice from the path. "A baby giraffe – and there's a girl stroking her!"

The zoo gates must have opened to the public while Zoe was working, because a family of visitors had walked up to the fence. A lady was pushing a bright-blue buggy with a toddler sitting inside, clapping his little hands happily. Next to them was a red-haired girl a bit younger than Zoe, wearing a giraffe T-shirt and holding her dad's hand. She was gazing in amazement at Zoe and Daisy. Zoe smiled at her, and Meep chattered a friendly greeting.

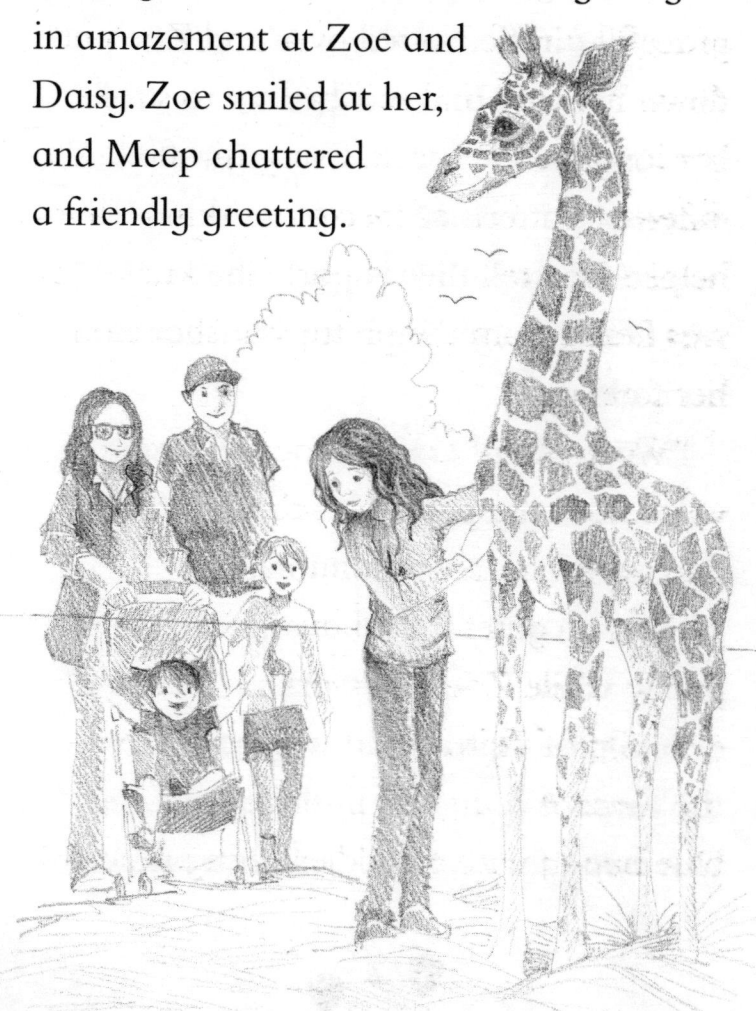

The girl smiled back shyly, her eyes wide. "Are you a zookeeper?" she asked Zoe.

Zoe giggled. "Maybe one day!" she said. "I'm Zoe, and this is Meep. My Great-Uncle Horace is the owner of the Rescue Zoo."

"Oh, you mean Horace Higgins! I've heard of him," said the girl's mum.

"He's a famous explorer, isn't he?" her dad added.

Zoe nodded. "He met so many hurt, lost or frightened animals on his adventures that he decided to build the Rescue Zoo. Now it's a safe place for any creature that needs a home," she explained. "Great-Uncle Horace still travels round the world looking for animals to help. Sometimes he's away for months, and we never know when he's going to come back.

"My mum's the Rescue Zoo vet. We live in a little cottage here in the zoo, so she can treat any animal whenever they need her. And I spend as much time with the animals as I can, especially at the weekends!"

"I can't believe you *live* here," the girl said wistfully. "You're so lucky."

"I know," said Zoe, beaming. She was very proud of her special home!

"And are the giraffes your favourites?" the girl's mum asked. "Amy here *loves* giraffes. She was so excited about seeing them, so this is the first enclosure we came to."

Zoe smiled. "Would you like to feed Daisy?" she asked. "She's already had lots of acacia leaves for breakfast but I have an apple here that you can give her as a treat."

Amy's mouth dropped open. "Really?" she breathed. "I would *love* to!"

Zoe reached into her pocket and passed a shiny green apple over the fence. Amy clutched it, looking nervous. "Just hold your arm out straight and keep your hand flat. She won't bite. She's really gentle," Zoe promised, smiling at Daisy.

Amy's dad pulled out his camera and started taking pictures as Amy held the apple out. Very carefully, Daisy bent down her long neck and sniffed the little girl's hand. Then she picked up the apple in one bite and started crunching it happily. Amy gasped. "Her nose is so soft!" she whispered.

"Did she come from somewhere in Africa?" Amy's dad asked.

Zoe shook her head. "Daisy's mum, Dolly, was rescued from Kenya. But Daisy was born here in the zoo, in the middle of the night. I was the first person to see her! Meep and I came to give Dolly her breakfast in the morning and there was Daisy – already walking around!"

When Amy had finished giving Daisy her treat, her dad ruffled her hair. "We'd better go and visit some of the other animals now, love. We've still got lots to see," he told her. "How about the hippos next?"

"We'll come back to see Daisy before we leave," her mum added.

Amy grinned at Zoe. "Thank you *so* much for letting me feed her. I loved it," she said, her cheeks pink with happiness.

The family walked off down the path, chatting excitedly. Zoe waited until they were out of sight, and sighed. "That was close!" she said to Daisy. "I didn't hear them walking up to the fence. It's lucky we weren't talking!"

Daisy nodded, and Meep squeaked in agreement. "They might have guessed our secret, Zoe!" the little lemur chirped.

Zoe grinned. Most people thought her life was amazing because she lived at the Rescue Zoo. But there was something else unusual about her – only this was a secret. On her sixth birthday Zoe had found out

that animals talk to people all the time!
Most people just hear squeaks, grunts,
roars and other animal noises. But some
people can understand everything they
say. Lucky, special people – like Zoe!

Chapter Two
A Double Delivery

"Come on, Meep!" said Zoe. "Let's head to the otter enclosure. Mum said the babies are getting a new toy this morning!"

Daisy bleated gently at Zoe, who smiled. "Of course we'll see you later," she promised, reaching out to stroke Daisy's soft muzzle. "Frankie told me you've been

playing chase with the rest of the herd,
and I want to come and watch."

Daisy bleated again and fluttered her
long, dark eyelashes. Zoe giggled and
nodded. "OK," she said. "If you're *very*
good, I might bring another apple with
me." The young giraffe grunted happily
and trotted back to the rest of the herd.

Zoe made sure the gate was safely
locked before heading down the path. It
was a warm autumn day and the zoo was
busy with visitors. Meep scampered along
in front of her, darting nimbly through the
crowds and along the top of the fences.
Some people pointed, and one lady
gasped, "Look! That monkey has escaped
from its enclosure!"

Zoe giggled. "Don't worry," she called.
"Meep's not a monkey, he's a lemur, and

he hasn't escaped. He's one of the most special animals at the Rescue Zoo and he's allowed to run free."

They passed the colourful kingfishers perched around their leafy lake home and the capuchin monkeys in their lush jungle. There was an especially big crowd gathered in front of the next enclosure. Luna was a beautiful arctic wolf with a soft, shaggy white coat, a jet-black nose and pale-blue eyes. Last month her gorgeous cubs had been born: a girl called Stella and a boy called Sam. Their home was a snowy clearing, surrounded by a circle of pine trees glittering with ice, with a gap at the front for visitors to look through. Luna and Sam were curled up asleep together, but little Stella was wide awake and playing happily with her mum's fluffy tail. When she saw Zoe she gave an excited bark and rushed up to the fence. Zoe waved at her. If the paths had been quieter she would have stopped to speak to the cub, but with so many visitors around it was too risky.

A little further along was another
beautiful enclosure – but this one was
empty. It was full of bamboo plants with
a waterfall trickling down a rocky cliff.
Three low wooden platforms were built
in the middle, connected by ladders and
ramps. This used to be the home of Su
Lin, the giant panda.

Zoe couldn't help feeling sad as she
walked past the empty enclosure. Su Lin
had died a few months ago. Zoe's mum
had explained that Su Lin wasn't hurt
or poorly – she was just very old. Zoe
had cried for ages but tried to remember
that Su Lin had loved her life at the
Rescue Zoo. She had been a gentle,
cuddly creature, full of funny stories about
growing up in China with her little sister,
Bai Yun. Zoe bit her lip and glanced at

Meep, who jumped into her arms for a
hug. They both missed the giant panda
very much.

Once they turned the corner and saw the otter enclosure ahead, Zoe felt more cheerful. Noisy squeaks of excitement were coming from their riverside home.

Zoe and Meep ran up to the fence, and Meep scampered on to Zoe's head for a better view. Jess, the otter keeper, was holding a yellow bouncy ball above her head. The baby otters, Otto and Benedict, were waiting on the riverbank, eagerly bobbing their sleek little heads up and down. Then Jess threw the ball into the water, and with a splash Otto and Benedict jumped straight after it! Otto

reached the ball first and sent it high up
into the air with a clever flick of his snout.
His brother squeaked happily and turned
a roly-poly under the water. "That looks
like fun!" Zoe called, laughing.

Suddenly Meep's ears pricked up.
"What's that noise, Zoe?" the little lemur
asked.

Zoe listened. Over the squeaks and
splashes of the otters she could hear a
strange honking sound.

"I don't know,
Meep," she said,
puzzled. "It's a
bit like when
some of the
geese caught
a cold last
year."

"Or when Oscar tied his trunk into
a knot by accident," Meep suggested,
giggling.

"I don't think it's an animal sound at
all," Zoe said thoughtfully. "It sounds
more like...a car horn playing a funny
tune. But how would anyone drive a car
into the Rescue Zoo? The paths aren't
wide enough!"

The noise was growing louder now,
and Zoe could hear the low grumble
of an engine. Otto and Benedict were
peering curiously over the fence, and in
the trees above them a flock of wild green
parakeets started squawking excitedly.

Suddenly a huge, gleaming motorbike
appeared from around the corner. With
another honk of its horn it sped down
the path towards them. The driver was

wearing a big, shiny helmet, a safari jacket and a pair of old-fashioned goggles. A white scarf was wrapped around his neck. Meep squeaked with joy and Zoe gasped. "Great-Uncle Horace!"

With a screech of brakes, the motorbike pulled up next to them. Its number plate said RESCUE 1 and it was covered with colourful stickers, showing all the places in the world that Great-Uncle Horace had visited. Attached to it was a bright-red sidecar with the hot-air balloon symbol of the Rescue Zoo painted on the side. A large and very grumpy-looking bird was perched inside it, her blue feathers fluffed up. Kiki was Great-Uncle Horace's hyacinth macaw, and they went everywhere together, just like Zoe and Meep!

Great-Uncle Horace lifted off his
goggles and beamed at them, his untidy
white hair sticking out from underneath
his helmet. "Zoe, my dear. And Meep, you
little rascal! It's wonderful to see you both.
I've missed you very much."

"Hooray! Hooray! Goo's back!"
chattered Meep. The funny little lemur
found it hard to say Great-Uncle

Horace's name so had made up his own version instead.

"We've missed you too," said Zoe, grinning. "I can't believe you're home, Great-Uncle Horace. We thought you were somewhere in Asia!"

"I *was* in Asia, my dear. Northern China, to be precise. And I've brought a very important delivery back to the zoo!" Great-Uncle Horace's eyes twinkled. "I came as fast as I could, by boat and then by bike. That's why Kiki here is rather cross. We drove along some very bumpy roads, you see. Motorbike is *not* her favourite way to travel."

Meep sniggered and Kiki gave a haughty squawk. The cheeky lemur and the proud old bird loved their owners but they didn't like each other very much!

"Naughty Meep," whispered Zoe.

"Anyway, my dear, hop on!" said Great-Uncle Horace.

"Where are we going?" Zoe asked. As she climbed on to the motorbike behind Great-Uncle Horace, with Meep on her shoulder, she spotted a large wooden crate tucked into the sidecar next to Kiki. What could it be? Great-Uncle Horace had mentioned *a very important delivery*. Zoe's heart leaped. *Please let it be a new animal for the Rescue Zoo!* she thought hopefully.

"Oh, not far," said Great-Uncle Horace, smiling mysteriously. "Hold tight!"

The engine roared and they raced back along the path. All around them the air was filled with happy squawks, whinnies and hoots as the news that Great-Uncle Horace was back spread through the zoo.

They turned the corner and parked
at the side of the path, underneath a
sprawling plum tree. "Zoe, look where
Goo has brought us," Meep whispered
in Zoe's ear.

"Su Lin's empty enclosure!" Zoe
gasped. She glanced at the wooden crate.
Suddenly her heart was racing with
excitement.

Great-Uncle Horace took off his helmet
and turned to Zoe. "I know you must be
wondering what I've brought home with
me, my dear," he said, smiling. "Well, it
is a new animal for the zoo – and we
already have the perfect home for it. Can
you guess what it is?"

Meep bounced up and down on Zoe's
shoulder. "I know! I know!" the little
lemur chirped.

Zoe took a deep, nervous breath. She thought she knew too – and she desperately hoped she was right. "Is it…is it a panda?" she asked, crossing her fingers tightly.

Great-Uncle Horace shook his head. Meep squeaked in surprise and Zoe's heart sank in disappointment. As soon as they had arrived at Su Lin's enclosure, she'd been *sure* it was a panda.

Then Zoe realised Great-Uncle Horace was chuckling softly. He climbed off the motorbike and helped Zoe and Meep down too. Kiki flew out of the sidecar and landed in the plum tree overhead, making a few golden leaves drift gently to the ground. Then Great-Uncle Horace reached over and opened the door of the wooden crate slightly. "Have a look," he told her.

Zoe peeped inside. It was warm and snug in the crate, and she could make out a fluffy black and white bundle. The bundle wriggled – and Zoe grinned in delight. There were *two* adorable creatures, cuddled up asleep together. "I can't believe it!" she cried. "It's not a panda. It's *two* pandas!"

"That's right!" said Great-Uncle Horace, beaming happily. "Two baby panda cubs. They're just three months old – and they're sisters. Zoe, meet the Rescue Zoo's first ever panda twins!"

Chapter Three
Zoe's Mistake

Zoe stared in delight at the fluffy bundles. One of the sleeping cubs rolled over and yawned, showing her tiny pink tongue, before snuggling back up against her sister.

"They're beautiful," Zoe said softly. "Where did they come from?"

"From another zoo," Great-Uncle

Horace explained. "Twin pandas are very rare indeed, Zoe. But it costs a lot of money to look after just one panda, because they need so much special care. The zoo could only afford to keep one cub, and was going to send her sister to a panda orphanage."

Zoe frowned. "But that's horrible! They're twins; they belong together."

"Exactly, my dear!" cried Great-Uncle Horace, nodding. "That's why I decided to bring them both to the Rescue Zoo. It was the only way to make sure they weren't split up." He glanced at the enclosure, then smiled at Zoe gently. "Besides, I knew how much everyone was missing Su Lin. Of course, the twins can never replace her. But when I had the chance to bring pandas back to the zoo,

I just had to take it!"

"I'm glad you did," Zoe replied, grinning. Meep chattered in agreement and Zoe smiled at her little friend.

"Well, I'd better tell everyone else," said Great-Uncle Horace. He rummaged around in the pockets of his safari jacket. Zoe giggled as he pulled out a ball of string, then a compass, and then a packet of his favourite custard-cream biscuits. In the largest pocket he found his battered old safari hat, which he jammed on to his head. Finally he held up what he had been looking for: a walkie-talkie.

"Come in, Rescue Zoo," he announced cheerily. "Horace speaking! I'm back, and I'm at the panda enclosure with Zoe and Meep. Come quickly, everyone. I've brought two panda cubs with me!"

There was a crackle, then all the zoo staff started replying. "Mr Higgins! That's fantastic news!" Zoe heard Jess say from the otter enclosure.

"I'll be there in a minute!" added the penguin keeper, Will.

The most excited reply was from Stephanie, the keeper who had looked after Su Lin. "Pandas?" she gasped. "Two of them? I can't believe it! Wait there – I'm coming straight over."

There was another crackle, and Zoe heard a familiar, happy voice. "Uncle Horace, I'm so pleased you're home," cried her mum, Lucy. "I'm on my way now. Don't run off on another adventure before I get there!"

Great-Uncle Horace chuckled. "Ah, there's my favourite niece. Don't worry, my dear. This time I'll be staying at the zoo for a few days, to help our new arrivals settle in."

Great-Uncle Horace turned back to Zoe. "Let's take the twins into their new home," he said. "They must be hungry. Did you know that pandas spend more than half of every day eating? And do you know what they love to eat more than anything else?"

"Bamboo!" Zoe said. Su Lin had munched through dozens of pieces of hard, green bamboo every day.

"That's right!" said Great-Uncle Horace. "Bamboo's a fascinating plant, Zoe. It grows very quickly indeed and there are more than three hundred different types. Here at the Rescue Zoo, we have just three kinds: umbrella, arrow and golden bamboo. Our new arrivals are still a little too young for bamboo though. For now, we'll feed them lots of nice, warm milk."

Carefully Great-Uncle Horace lifted the crate out of the sidecar and carried it over to the enclosure. Zoe opened the gate with her paw-print charm and they all went inside. Most of the Rescue Zoo's enclosures were kept neat and tidy, but this one had become very overgrown since Su Lin died. Chinese wild flowers had sprung up among the trees, and with no one there to nibble the bamboo plants they'd grown right up to the top of the fence.

"Goodness!" exclaimed Great-Uncle Horace. "It feels very wild indeed, as if we really are in the Chinese mountains.

How lovely! Now, let's see what our new
arrivals think."

He put the crate down and opened
the door all the way, so it rested on the
ground. Then he stepped back and waited.
Zoe watched the crate and tried not to
fidget. When an animal was seeing its
new home for the first time, the Rescue
Zoo staff were always as quiet and still as
possible. That way, the animal wouldn't
be frightened. Zoe didn't move, even
though she was so excited, but naughty
Meep couldn't be still for a second and
hopped up and down, desperate to see
what the pandas did.

Everything was quiet. Then there was a
curious squeak from inside the crate. The
cubs had noticed the open door!

Suddenly a little face appeared in the

doorway. Zoe gasped as she saw the first cub, now wide awake. Her face and body were as white and fluffy as a cloud. Her ears, arms and legs were black, and there was a ring of black fur around each of her bright, curious eyes. Her black nose twitched, and she scampered out of the crate excitedly.

"I think she likes it, don't you?" whispered Great-Uncle Horace, beaming.

Zoe nodded, unable to tear her eyes away
from the beautiful animal.

Then the second cub peeped out shyly.
She was a bit smaller than her sister, with
a black splodge on her tummy. She gazed
at the lush trees, the glittering waterfall
and the tall bamboo plants. Then she put
her little head to one side and curiously
squeaked a question.

"Yes, that's right!"
Zoe burst out
excitedly.
"This is your
new home –
the Rescue
Zoo."

Both
cubs stared
at her in

surprise. By her feet, Meep squealed in horror. "Zoe, shhhh!" the little lemur hissed. "Goo's here!"

Zoe clapped her hand tightly over her mouth, as if she could somehow make the words disappear. Suddenly her heart was racing. She couldn't *believe* she'd made such a silly mistake. *She had talked to the pandas in front of Great-Uncle Horace!*

Chapter Four
A Lucky Escape

Zoe looked quickly at Great-Uncle
Horace. She had never spoken to an
animal in front of another person
before, but she'd been so excited about
the pandas, she'd forgotten Great-
Uncle Horace was there! She thought
desperately, trying not to panic. What
could she say to explain? Maybe she

could pretend she'd muddled up her words?

But Great-Uncle Horace didn't seem to have heard her. There was a funny smile on his face, but he was still watching the cubs look round their new home. Zoe let out a deep, shaky breath. *That was a lucky escape!* she thought. *I need to be more careful.*

"Gosh, Zoe, you look very serious," cried a voice from behind her. "Cheer up, sweetheart! This is the best day we've had at Rescue Zoo in ages. I can't believe we've got panda twins!"

It was Stephanie, Su Lin's old keeper, her freckled face pink from rushing along the path. Her chestnut-brown hair was tied up in a bun and she was wearing the blue Rescue Zoo uniform with a golden hot-air balloon sewn on the pocket. She grinned in delight, crouching down to stroke the smaller cub's soft fur. "Aren't they *gorgeous*! I don't think I've ever seen such small pandas before."

Will, Jess and Frankie all rushed down the path together. Then Lucy arrived with some of the other zookeepers, looking very out of breath. "The zoo visitors must be wondering what's going on!" she laughed, hugging Great-Uncle Horace. "The animals are making such a lot of noise, and all the zoo staff are dashing along the path as if they're running a race!"

"This is impossible," spluttered a voice from behind them. "*Two* new pandas? That's twice the money. *And* twice the mess!"

Zoe turned, her heart sinking. Mr

Pinch, the zoo manager, was standing by the gate, his skinny arms folded tightly. His uniform was crisply ironed and his shoes perfectly polished, but his thin face was as sour as vinegar.

Only horrid Mr Pinch could be grumpy about such gorgeous creatures arriving at the zoo! thought Zoe.

"Ah, Mr Pinch! A pleasure as always," Great-Uncle Horace called, his eyes twinkling. "I see you've come to meet our new arrivals."

"Mr Higgins, *delightful* to have you back, of course," Mr Pinch added quickly, his cheeks flushing pink. "But perhaps we should discuss this before we do anything *hasty*. I really do not see how the pandas can stay here. One cub would be very expensive, but *two*—"

"Yes, two!" Great-Uncle Horace interrupted cheerfully. "Two pandas, who *both* need a home. Remember, the Rescue Zoo never turns an animal away – no matter what."

Mr Pinch went the colour of a ripe tomato. "Well, no," he snapped. "But the cost—"

"We'll think of something!" Great-Uncle Horace told him, walking over to the flustered zoo manager and patting his shoulder. "Let's go to my office for a chat. I know you must have some excellent ideas up your sleeve! Besides, it's time I had a cup of tea and a custard cream. Come along, Kiki. See you later, everyone." He marched away down the path, with Kiki soaring above him. Mr Pinch shot the pandas a final cross look and then followed, grumbling under his breath.

Stephanie jumped to her feet. "Right, everyone! Let's get this enclosure fixed up for the cubs."

The zookeepers set to work. Frankie fetched some fresh wood chippings for the ground, while Jess found a pile of warm, fleecy blankets for the cubs to sleep on. Everyone else swept away the piles of autumn leaves and cut the sprawling ivy off the wooden platforms.

Meanwhile, Zoe's mum checked the cubs to make sure they were both healthy.

As Zoe held each cub carefully in her lap, Lucy used the stethoscope around her neck to listen to their heartbeats.

Then she opened the special vet bag she always carried and shone a small torch into their eyes and ears. "They're both perfect," she told Zoe, smiling. "This one here is a little bit bigger than her sister, but that happens quite often when two babies are born at the same time."

Soon there was only one job left. "We need to mend the wooden fence around the enclosure," said Stephanie. "Some of the wood has rotted away, and the bamboo has grown so much that it's pushed holes right through it!"

Will and Jess fetched some new pieces of wood and some nails from the zoo storehouse, and used them to patch up the holes in the fence.

Finally all the work was done, and the twins' enclosure looked as good as new. "Thanks for your help, everyone!" called Stephanie as the keepers left in small groups, chatting about the adorable cubs.

Lucy gave Zoe a kiss before heading back to the zoo hospital. "I've got to check on a poorly raccoon, and give some medicine to an aardvark with a sore

snout," she said. "I expect you and Meep
will be here all day! Just be home in time
for tea."

As Lucy set off down the path,
Stephanie grinned at Zoe. "I think it's
lunchtime for hungry panda cubs!" she
announced. "I'll fetch some milk. Will you
watch them until I'm back?"

"Of course!" said Zoe quickly. She
caught Meep's eye and the little lemur
chirped excitedly. Being alone with the
cubs meant she'd be able to talk to them
– with no one else around this time! As
soon as Stephanie left the enclosure, she
knelt down. The bigger cub was playing
happily with a piece of twig while her
sister was quietly watching a worm
wriggle along the ground.

"Hello!" she said softly. "I'm Zoe and

this is my best friend, Meep. What are your names?"

The bigger cub looked up and squeaked in surprise. Zoe giggled. "Yes, that's right – I *can* talk to animals. You weren't imagining it! I wasn't supposed to do it before though. I forgot my great-uncle was there."

The cub squeaked again, eagerly. "Chi Chi," Zoe said, nodding. "That's such a pretty name. What about you, little one?"

The smaller cub blinked at her, then squealed shyly. "Mei Mei," repeated Zoe, smiling gently at her. "We're so pleased you've come to the Rescue Zoo. We're going to look after you here, I promise."

Meep chattered a warning as Stephanie came back into the enclosure. "Zoe, do you want to feed one of the cubs?" she asked, holding up two bottles of warm milk. "I know you're an expert!"

Zoe grinned happily. "Yes, *please!*" she said, taking a bottle from Stephanie. She loved feeding baby animals!

Carefully she picked up Mei Mei and held the little panda against her chest. With a tiny squeak, Mei Mei cuddled up against Zoe. Her fur was so soft and fluffy, and she felt very warm. Zoe offered her the bottle and Mei Mei started drinking the milk happily.

Stephanie smiled as she fed Chi Chi. "We're so lucky to have them here, you know," she told Zoe. "Pandas are some of the most endangered animals in the world. There are fewer than two thousand living in the wild now."

Zoe frowned. She knew that sounded like a big number but it was actually very low. There were almost a thousand people in her school, and that was the same as half all the pandas living wild in the whole wide world. "Why aren't there more?" she asked.

"There are lots of reasons," Stephanie explained. "Poachers hunt pandas because they can sell their fur for lots of money. Pandas need to eat so much bamboo that it's really hard for them to find homes with enough plants growing nearby. Plus, pandas don't have babies very often – and twins are especially unusual."

Chi Chi finished her milk and gave a little hiccup. Stephanie laughed. "They certainly enjoyed that!" she said, tickling the cub's fluffy belly.

"I've thought of some names, Stephanie," said Zoe. "What about Chi Chi for that cub, and Mei Mei for this one?"

"Those are perfect!" Stephanie exclaimed. "In Chinese, 'Mei Mei' means 'little sister'. How did you know that?"

Zoe thought quickly. "I...I learned it at school," she explained, hoping she wasn't blushing. Zoe didn't like making up stories but sometimes it was the only way to cover up her secret. She couldn't tell Stephanie that the baby pandas had told her their names!

When Mei Mei had finished her bottle, Zoe and Stephanie put both pandas down. Straightaway, Chi Chi was ready to explore. She scampered over to the nearest wooden platform and clambered up the ramp, with a little help from Stephanie. At the top, she squeaked happily, excited to see her new home from high up. Then she padded back down the ramp and dashed over to the waterfall. "You're going to be a little handful, Chi Chi. I can tell already!" Stephanie laughed, chasing after her.

Zoe glanced down curiously at Mei Mei, who had crept on to her lap. The smaller panda watched her sister quietly but didn't seem to want to join in. "Don't you want to explore, Mei Mei?" Zoe whispered, but the cub shook her head.

A moment later Chi Chi came charging back through the enclosure and nudged her little sister with her front paws, squeaking bossily. Mei Mei cuddled closer to Zoe and whimpered. Stephanie scratched her head. "It's funny that they're not playing together," she said, puzzled. "They must have been cooped up together for too long. They just need a little bit of space and they'll be rolling around together soon enough."

But Zoe and Meep looked at each other in alarm. They had understood Chi Chi and Mei Mei's panda noises, and knew what was wrong. Chi Chi thought her sister was a baby because she didn't want to explore and play. Mei Mei didn't want to do the scary things Chi Chi did, and thought her sister was a show-off.

Oh no! The panda twins didn't seem to like each other at all!

Chapter Five
Squabbling Sisters

As Zoe got ready for bed that evening she couldn't stop worrying about the little pandas. All afternoon the sisters had squabbled. Zoe had encouraged them to play together but energetic Chi Chi had just squeaked crossly at quiet Mei Mei, who was still feeling nervous in her new home. Stephanie had been disappointed, and even Great-Uncle Horace had looked concerned when he popped over to the cottage to say goodnight. "We'll try again tomorrow," he'd said reassuringly. "Perhaps the twins are tired after travelling such a long way."

Zoe brushed her teeth, put on her orange tiger-striped pyjamas and climbed into bed. Meep was already curled up on her pillow. The little lemur looked worried too. Zoe switched off the dolphin lamp next to her bed and sighed. "What are we going to do, Meep? Great-Uncle Horace brought the sisters to the Rescue Zoo so they could stay together but they just don't get along."

"But *why*, Zoe?" Meep asked, his little nose wrinkled up anxiously. "I don't understand."

"I think it's because they're so different," Zoe said thoughtfully. "Chi Chi is playful and adventurous, while Mei Mei's timid and quiet. They're so lucky though," she added. "I'd *love* to have a sister or a brother, even if we were really different! Someone I could always play with, and tell all my problems and secrets."

"But you have me, Zoe!" Meep chattered happily, snuggling up against her. "We play together lots. *And* I already know your biggest secret!"

Zoe laughed and pulled Meep close for a cuddle. "That's true, Meep. I don't need anyone else when I've got you!" She rubbed her cheek against his furry head. "But the pandas *do* need each other. Tomorrow we have to find a way to help them get along!"

The next morning Zoe ran out of the cottage as soon as she'd eaten a quick bowl of muesli and Meep had munched a banana. Zoe was desperate to get to the panda enclosure early, before the visitors started arriving.

"Maybe the pandas will be playing together when we get there," Meep chirped brightly as they dashed along the path. Zoe hoped her little friend was right.

As they stepped into the enclosure, Zoe saw Mei Mei padding curiously up to the waterfall. "Look, Meep!" Zoe whispered. "She's finally feeling brave enough to explore!"

Then Chi Chi noticed what her sister was doing. With a happy squeal, Chi Chi scrambled towards Mei Mei and bumped playfully into her. Poor Mei Mei wobbled ...and fell underneath the waterfall with a big splash! "Naughty Chi Chi," Zoe muttered as the older cub scampered quickly away, and Mei Mei gave a cross squeak. "That's no way to make friends."

Stephanie had just arrived at the enclosure. "Morning, Zoe," she called.

"Could you grab a blanket from the pandas' sleeping area? We'll need to dry Mei Mei. I'm afraid the cubs still aren't getting along."

Zoe fetched a fluffy blanket as a very wet Mei Mei padded over. She scooped the panda up and rubbed her fur gently with the blanket. "There, you're nice and dry," she soothed, making sure she spoke too quietly for Stephanie to hear. "Chi Chi was just playing."

Stephanie sighed. "It's such a shame. Both cubs seem to love their new home. Chi Chi adores the wooden platforms and the ramps, and even Mei Mei's starting to settle in. But if they don't make friends soon..." She hesitated.

"Then what will happen?" Zoe asked at once.

"We'll have to split them up," Stephanie explained. "While they're little they can't do any harm, but when they're fully grown they might hurt each other."

"But we'd be able to keep them both at the zoo, wouldn't we?" Zoe asked anxiously. "One could stay here and the other could go in a different enclosure."

Stephanie shook her head sadly. "I'm afraid not, sweetheart. We don't have any spare enclosures big enough for an adult panda. They need *lots* of space, you see. One sister would probably have to go to another zoo."

Zoe's heart sank. It was horrible to imagine the sisters not liking each other, and it was even worse to think about them being separated. What if one of the twins was sent back to China? That was thousands of miles away. They would never see each other again.

Suddenly Zoe remembered something. *Su Lin*. Her old friend had loved telling stories about her little sister and all the fun they'd had together. Su Lin and Bai Yun had been separated when they were still very young. But Su Lin had *never* stopped missing Bai Yun, even years later. Zoe took a deep, determined breath. She was *not* going to let that happen to Chi Chi and Mei Mei. She had to make them see how lucky they were to have each other.

Stephanie gave her hand a gentle squeeze. "I'm sorry, Zoe. I didn't mean to worry you," she said. "Listen, cheer up. It's breakfast time and we're going to try giving the cubs some solid food today."

She had brought a small plastic box with her that morning, and took the lid off. It was full of apple and bamboo, sliced up into tiny chunks. "It might seem silly to bring bamboo when there's so much growing around us," she said. "But until the babies' teeth grow stronger, it's very hard for them to bite into. I cut up the softest, freshest piece I could find, to make it easier for them."

She gave the box a little shake. Chi Chi's black nose twitched and she scampered towards them, excited by the smell of the juicy bamboo. Mei Mei looked curious too, and followed cautiously.

Stephanie glanced down at her watch. "Oh dear. I've just remembered – I'm supposed to be over at Alex's enclosure in

five minutes. He hasn't had his breakfast
bananas yet, and you know how grumpy
the old gorilla gets when he's hungry!"

"I can feed the pandas!" Zoe offered
quickly, winking at Meep. The little lemur
chirped. They both knew the more time
they could spend alone with the cubs, the
more chance they had of helping them
make friends with each other.

Stephanie beamed at her. "Are you
sure? Zoe, you're a star. I'll be back really
soon."

Stephanie handed the plastic box to
Zoe and dashed out of the enclosure.
When she was out of sight, Zoe glanced
around, making sure no one else was on
the path nearby. Then she crouched down
and tipped a few slices of bamboo into
her palm. "Come on, you two!" she said

softly. "Are you hungry?"

Both cubs nodded their heads eagerly.
Zoe smiled. "I've got lots of tasty treats for
you," she told them. "But this bamboo is
only for pandas
who behave
nicely."

The cubs
blinked
innocently
up at her.
*I hope that
worked!*
thought Zoe.
Carefully she handed one piece of
bamboo to each twin. They both grasped
the pieces in their paws, sniffed at them
and then started to nibble. A moment
later Chi Chi squeaked happily, and

Mei Mei's dark eyes went wide with delight.

Zoe giggled. This was the first time the pandas had ever tried bamboo – and they loved it! And for the first time that morning they weren't fighting.

But it didn't last very long. As soon as naughty Chi Chi finished her bamboo she reached over and grabbed Mei Mei's piece out of her paws and gobbled it up! Mei Mei turned to Zoe and wailed.

"No, that *wasn't* very fair of Chi Chi," admitted Zoe. "But it's all right, there's lots more bamboo for you both."

But the older panda was just as cross now! Chi Chi thumped her little paw on the ground and squeaked indignantly.

"Chi Chi! Calling your sister a telltale isn't very nice," scolded Zoe, feeling more and more worried. "Come on, there's no need to fall out. Why don't you try a piece of apple this time?"

But the cubs had forgotten all about their treats and suddenly Zoe couldn't get a word in over their angry squabbling. Her heart sank even further as Chi Chi pushed her sister over. The playful panda was very naughty!

Meep chirped a sudden warning and from behind her Zoe heard a loud, sneering voice. "Fussing and fighting already, I see. I just *knew* those pandas would be trouble."

Zoe groaned quietly as horrid Mr Pinch marched into the enclosure. This morning was getting worse and worse!

Chapter Six
Double Trouble

Mr Pinch peered snootily round the
enclosure. "I was expecting to find a real,
grown-up zookeeper here," he announced,
narrowing his eyes at Zoe.

Meep leaped on to Zoe's shoulder and
chattered angrily, and Zoe shot her little
friend a warning look. Mr Pinch did not
approve of Zoe and Meep wandering

freely around the zoo and all the enclosures. Even when they were trying to help, he would grumble, "Miss Parker, this is a job for *zoo staff* – not a little girl and a naughty lemur!"

"Stephanie went to give Alex his breakfast," Zoe told Mr Pinch politely. "I promised to stay and watch the cubs while she was gone."

Just then Chi Chi let out an especially noisy squeal and thumped Mei Mei with her little paw. Mr Pinch glared at the bickering pandas down his long, thin nose. "I've heard all about the pandas fighting," he announced. "I *told* Mr Higgins they would be a nuisance! But they won't be causing trouble in my zoo for long." He nodded his head bossily. "Mr Higgins wants there to be a special event

on Friday, to welcome the pandas to the
Rescue Zoo. Lots of important people
will be there: visitors, news reporters, even
the mayor! I won't have the cubs being
bothersome in front of them. If they are
still fighting by then, I'll start proceedings
to send one of them to another zoo."

Meep gave a squeak of alarm, and
Zoe stared at Mr Pinch in horror. "But –
but Friday is just a few days away!" she
stammered, glancing at the squabbling
cubs. It seemed almost impossible that
they would make friends by then.

"Well, they'd better start getting along
quickly!" Mr Pinch told her nastily. "Now,
I've come to take some photos of the cubs
so I can make posters for the event. I'd
better get started. I'm *very* busy, as usual."
He pulled a camera out of his pocket and

pointed at Chi Chi. "That one first."

He stepped over to the little panda. But as he held the camera up to his face, Chi Chi rolled away from him with a playful squeal.

"Sit still!" Mr Pinch snapped.

He moved towards Chi Chi again. But the cub gave another excited squeak and scampered quickly around Mr Pinch, so that she was perched behind him. Mr Pinch whirled round crossly – and cheeky Chi Chi turned a roly-poly through his legs, landing right back where she'd started!

"That's enough!" Mr Pinch spluttered, suddenly looking very hot and red. "I will *not* stand for such rude behaviour. I am the *zoo manager*! Well, if *you* won't behave, I'll take a photo of your sister first."

He turned to Mei Mei, who gazed up
at him quietly. Next to bold, naughty Chi
Chi she looked so timid and well behaved,
so what happened next was even more of
a surprise. The little panda poked her tiny
pink tongue out at Mr Pinch!

Chi Chi let out a delighted squeak
of laughter at her sister being naughty.
She scrambled over to Mei Mei and
playfully rolled her around on the ground,
squealing happily. When they sat up
again they were covered in dirt, mud
and bits of twig. Mr Pinch stared angrily
at them. "Naughty, messy creatures," he
fumed. "I can't tell them apart now!"

Zoe looked at the cubs. *She* knew which
fluffy bundle was Chi Chi and which
was Mei Mei – even though the splodge
on Mei Mei's tummy was hidden by

the mud! But something was different about them. The cubs were huddled close, whispering to each other. Their eyes were bright and excited. *They're having fun together*, Zoe realised, suddenly feeling hopeful. *They're really getting along. And it's because they both love causing trouble for Mr Pinch!*

The zoo manager scowled at her, his

face very pink. "Which one is which?" he snapped. "I don't have all day."

"That's Chi Chi," Zoe said, pointing. "She's the older twin. And that's Mei Mei. She's a tiny bit smaller than her sister."

"Well, they're both just as troublesome as each other, if you ask me," Mr Pinch grumbled. "Now, where's my camera? I dropped it over here somewhere."

He turned round to pick up the camera, muttering crossly. While he was looking away, Mei Mei leaned over to squeak in her sister's ear. Chi Chi giggled...and just before Mr Pinch turned back the twins swapped places!

Meep squealed with laughter and Zoe couldn't help smiling. The cheeky pandas were just too funny, and she was so relieved to see them starting to make friends. Mr Pinch narrowed his eyes at her suspiciously. "You'd better not be tricking me," he warned her. "If you are, you'll be in big trouble!"

"I'm not tricking you, I promise," Zoe said truthfully. *After all*, she thought, *I did tell you the truth. It wasn't my fault the babies switched!*

Mr Pinch scowled at the muddy pandas. "Now the little pests are going to be all dirty on my posters," he grumbled.

He held up the camera again. Straightaway the cubs took off! Chi Chi scampered playfully in one direction, towards the waterfall. Mei Mei padded the other way, past the wooden platforms.

"Come back here this instant!" Mr Pinch shouted. But the cubs tumbled from one part of the enclosure to another and

never stayed still long enough for the furious zoo manager to take their photos.

Mr Pinch chased them until he was gasping for breath. Eventually he threw his hands in the air. His hat was tipped crookedly over one eye and his face was red and hot. "I give up!" he snapped. "Never, in all my years as manager of the Rescue Zoo, have I seen such naughty behaviour. I'll be informing Mr Higgins about this."

He stormed out of the enclosure and down the path, muttering fiercely under his breath. As soon as he turned the corner, Zoe and Meep looked at each other and giggled. "That was so much fun," the little lemur chattered gleefully. "Horrid old Pinch was as red as a raspberry!"

Zoe grinned happily. Together the twins were double trouble! But she didn't mind. All that mattered was that the sisters were starting to get along, and as long as they were friends they could *both* stay at the Rescue Zoo. She just hoped it would last.

"Chi Chi! Mei Mei!" she called. "He's gone! Come and finish your breakfast now."

The pandas bounded back over, and she bent down to give them both a cuddle. Chi Chi squeaked brightly up at her. Zoe laughed. "Yes, it looked like you were enjoying yourself!" she told the cheeky little cub.

She shared out the rest of the apple and bamboo and held her breath, hoping the cubs would nibble their treats happily this time. But her heart sank as naughty

Chi Chi snatched her sister's apple and scrambled playfully away with it, while Mei Mei gave a cross little squeak. Chi Chi grumbled that Mei Mei was no fun – and suddenly the pandas were fighting all over again.

"They're still not getting along, Meep," groaned Zoe. "I can't believe it. I thought they were starting to make friends, but that was only when they were having fun teasing Mr Pinch. Now that he's gone, they're falling out just like before."

She glanced at the older cub, who was splashing around in the waterfall. "Chi Chi just wants to play and be naughty. She doesn't understand that Mei Mei is quieter and doesn't always want to join in."

Meep's little nose wrinkled up anxiously. "What shall we do, Zoe?" he chirped.

Zoe bit her lip, feeling very worried. "We'd better go and find Stephanie and tell her what Mr Pinch said. This is really serious. If the babies don't make friends before Friday, one of them will be sent away. We can't let that happen!"

Chapter Seven
Missing Mei Mei

On Friday, Zoe flew into the cottage and dropped her school bag on the kitchen table. "Meep!" she called breathlessly. "I'm back. I ran all the way home!"

There was a tiny squeak from the bowl of bananas on the worktop. Then Meep's furry little head popped up, munching away. "Meep, you're supposed to *peel* the

bananas
before you
eat them!"
Zoe told
her friend,
gathering
him up for a
cuddle. "Come
on, let's go straight
to the panda enclosure.
Today's the special welcome event! Lots
of important people will be arriving soon,
all wanting to meet Chi Chi and Mei
Mei – and Mr Pinch will be watching to
see if they're getting along."

Meep's golden eyes were wide with
worry. "I peeped into their enclosure at
lunchtime, Zoe. They were still fighting!"
the little lemur told her.

Zoe sighed. "They haven't stopped fighting all week, Meep. I think this is our last chance to make them friends."

She ran up to her bedroom and quickly swapped her uniform for jeans and a warm red jumper, and pushed a ball into her backpack. Otto and Benedict had loved playing with a ball; maybe Chi Chi and Mei Mei would too? As they set off into the zoo, Zoe sighed. Every day that week, as soon as she'd arrived home from school, she and Meep had raced to visit Chi Chi and Mei Mei. They had tried everything they could think of to make the cubs get along but nothing seemed to work.

Once, Stephanie had let Zoe bring an old tyre into the enclosure for the sisters to play with. Chi Chi had loved it, but Mei Mei gave a frightened squeak whenever it rolled near her and Chi Chi had called her a baby. Another time Zoe had suggested they try a quiet game of sleeping logs. Mei Mei's eyes had lit up, but Chi Chi snorted that it sounded boring. Yesterday Zoe had tried explaining how important it was that they make friends but Mei Mei didn't seem to understand, and Chi Chi was too busy rolling in the mud to listen. Zoe hoped the ball worked – she wasn't sure what else to try.

The only time the twins had fun together was when Mr Pinch came to their enclosure. He had tried to take photos of them for his posters every day that week, and became crosser and crosser each time. As soon as he appeared, the twins would whisper mischievously and hide from him until he stomped away. In the end, Mr Pinch had to make do with some blurry pictures of Chi Chi's paw and Mei Mei's ear, which he was very grumpy about.

It was a sunny afternoon and the zoo was full of visitors enjoying themselves. As Zoe and Meep reached the panda enclosure, a crowd of little girls was gathered outside, one of them holding a birthday balloon and wearing a sparkly badge. "Look at the little panda – he's so cute!" she told her friends. "But I thought there were two? Mummy told me there were twin pandas."

"I can only see one," another girl agreed, standing on tiptoes to have a better look.

Zoe glanced over the fence. Chi Chi was huddled by herself in front of a big clump of bamboo next to the fence at the edge of the enclosure. "Mei Mei must be hiding from Mr Pinch again," she whispered to Meep. "But why does Chi Chi look so sad? That's not like her."

The party of girls took some pictures of themselves standing next to the fence, with Chi Chi in the background. As they rushed off to visit the hippos, Zoe pulled out her paw-print necklace and opened the gate. "Chi Chi, it's us!" she called softly as they stepped inside. "Is everything all right? Where's Mei Mei?"

As she heard Zoe's voice, Chi Chi looked up and let out a miserable whimper. Zoe and Meep hurried over to the little panda and Zoe knelt down beside her. "What do you mean, Mei Mei's gone?" she asked. "Where?"

Chi Chi sniffled sadly and crept behind the big clump of bamboo. Zoe peered after her and gasped. The bamboo was covering a big hole in the fence – a hole that the zookeepers hadn't patched up. And Mei Mei had disappeared through it!

Chapter Eight
Panda Panic

Zoe gazed in horror at the hole. "I don't understand, Chi Chi," she said, panic spreading through her tummy. "Mei Mei's so shy. Why did she escape?"

Chi Chi gulped and gave a little squeak. Zoe listened carefully as the little cub explained what had happened. When timid Mei Mei had found the hole in the fence, she'd decided to prove to her sister that she *wasn't* a baby. She was going to squeeze through it and explore the rest of the zoo! But bold, brave Chi Chi had been too frightened to follow.

Meep scampered over to the baby panda and gave her a comforting cuddle, while Zoe stroked her soft little head. "It's all right," she told her, trying not to let Chi Chi see how worried she was. "Mei Mei can't have gone very far. We'll find her, I promise."

Suddenly she heard a familiar, bossy voice coming down the path. "This way, this way! Follow me, everyone!" Mr Pinch called loudly. "The pandas are just around this corner."

Quickly, Zoe and Meep squeezed behind the bamboo with Chi Chi, so that they couldn't be seen from the path. A huge, chattering crowd of people was gathering outside the enclosure to meet the pandas. Lots of them were wearing important-looking badges, and some of them carried microphones or big TV cameras. Stephanie was there too, peering anxiously over the fence to see if the pandas were fighting or not.

"So where are they?" asked a reporter with big square glasses and a green tie. "I can't see either of them!"

"They're probably just having a little snooze somewhere," explained Stephanie. "Baby pandas as young as Chi Chi and Mei Mei need lots of sleep."

"Ahem! Yes, well, *I* knew that, of course," Mr Pinch interrupted pompously.

Zoe's mind was racing. She had to act fast, before Mr Pinch decided to come into the enclosure and start looking for the cubs. "Meep, we've got to find Mei Mei. She's only small, and with such a big crowd of people here she must be frightened," she whispered to the little lemur.

"Maybe we should ask all those people to look for her too?" Meep suggested.

Zoe shook her head. "We can't let anyone know Mei Mei's not in her enclosure. If the reporters find out a rare baby panda has managed to escape, it would be a disaster for the Rescue Zoo!"

She turned to Chi Chi. "Stay here, and we'll go and search for Mei Mei."

But the little panda shook her head stubbornly and squeaked. Zoe hesitated. "You can't come with me, Chi Chi. What if someone saw you?"

Chi Chi squeaked again and nudged her little nose against Zoe's backpack. Zoe couldn't help smiling. "OK – as long as you promise to stay very quiet and don't pop your head out. And no tickling me!"

Zoe emptied out the backpack and let Chi Chi wriggle inside. Taking a deep breath, she crept towards the gate, trying to stay hidden behind trees and huge bamboo plants so that the crowd wouldn't notice her. "It's lucky the enclosure is still so wild and overgrown!" she whispered to Meep.

Just then one of the reporters shouted, "I think I can see them! Over there, by that wooden platform!"

As the crowd was distracted, Zoe slipped out of the gate and back on to the path.

Just as she was about to start searching, someone tapped her on the shoulder.

"Zoe!" said a relieved voice. "Just the person I was hoping to see. How was school today?"

Zoe whirled round. "Mum!" she stammered, desperately hoping Lucy wouldn't ask what was in her backpack, or see it wriggling. "Er — school was fine."

"Listen, love, I need you to help me," said Lucy. "I was on my way to the gazelle enclosure with some medicine for Gordon's poorly tummy, but I've just had an urgent call on my walkie-talkie. One of the brown bear cubs has a thorn stuck in his paw and I need to take him straight to the zoo hospital. The poor little thing's very upset! Could you take the medicine instead?" She pulled a small bottle from the special vet bag she always carried, and passed it to Zoe.

Zoe's heart sank, but she nodded. As Lucy hurried off, Zoe whispered urgently to Meep, "Start telling all the animals about the missing cub. Ask them to help spread the word! Oscar can sound the alarm with his giant trunk, and the birds can fly around and search from the sky. We'll meet back here in five minutes. There's no time to lose!"

Chapter Nine
The Search is On

Zoe didn't think she'd ever run so fast. Clutching the medicine in one hand, she raced through the zoo, dodging and weaving past visitors. She could feel the backpack bumping against her back as she sped along, and hoped she wasn't making Chi Chi dizzy. "Excuse me!" she panted breathlessly. "Animal emergency!"

Her heart was thumping hard in her chest when she reached the grassy plain next to the lake, where the gazelles grazed. "Ah, Zoe!" called the gazelle keeper, waving. "Your mum said you'd be bringing—"

"Really sorry!" Zoe gasped, flinging the bottle into his hands and sprinting off again. "Can't stop now!"

Zoe raced around the zoo, calling out to the animals. The news of the escaped cub was spreading quickly. The zebras stamped their hooves and whinnied the message to their neighbours, the alpine hares. The flamingos flapped their wings and hooted to the wolves, who howled so loudly that every animal in the zoo could hear them. The warthogs snuffled around in their cool mud holes to make

sure Mei Mei wasn't there. The baboons checked in the bushes, and one of the crocodiles politely asked Zoe what the missing panda looked like. Zoe unzipped her backpack so Chi Chi could peep out. "Exactly like this!" she replied, holding the little cub up in the air. But it was no good, no one had seen Mei Mei.

They were almost back at the panda enclosure when Meep came scampering round the corner to meet them. "Everyone's looking for Mei Mei but there's no sign of her anywhere," he chattered. "What shall we do next?"

Zoe bit her lip and thought. "Let's go back to the enclosure again," she suggested. "We'll look for paw prints near the hole in the fence, or any other clue that might lead us to Mei Mei."

Chi Chi squeaked eagerly in agreement. Zoe zipped up her backpack and they crept along to the panda enclosure. There was a grumble of voices as they arrived. The crowd was getting restless and cross. Zoe saw the reporter with the glasses check his watch and shake his head. "How long do we have to wait to see these pandas?" he complained.

Suddenly a blur of deep-blue feathers swooped past his head, making him jump. Kiki landed on top of the fence and fluttered her wings as Great-Uncle Horace strolled down the path, crunching on a custard cream. "Good afternoon, everyone!" he called cheerily, tipping his explorer's hat to the crowd. "It's wonderful that you've all come to meet our special new arrivals!"

One of the reporters sighed loudly. "Well, we haven't met them yet," he moaned. "We haven't even caught a glimpse of them. I'm going home if they don't show up soon!"

"Oh, what a pity," Great-Uncle Horace said with concern. "You really must wait and see them. Pandas are so rare, especially twins." He smiled brightly at the man. "Did you know that in China they are called 'giant bear cats'? Some people also call them 'bamboo bears'. Fascinating!"

The crowd gathered round Great-Uncle Horace as he began telling them all about pandas. Even the grumpy reporter looked interested. Zoe knew he'd only be distracted for a few minutes though. She had to find Mei Mei and get both cubs back into their home – fast!

Quietly, she tiptoed round the outside of the enclosure until she found where the hole in the fence was hidden. Chi Chi started wriggling so much in the backpack that Zoe let her out. Together, Zoe, Meep and Chi Chi all began looking around for any sign of Mei Mei. Then Chi Chi squealed eagerly.

"What have you found, Chi Chi?" chirped Meep, hopping up and down.

Chi Chi lifted her paw and pointed. A wisp of white fluff was caught on the branch of a tall oak tree, just outside the enclosure. With an excited squeak, Chi Chi scampered up the tree.

"Chi Chi!" Zoe called in a loud whisper. It was just like naughty Chi Chi to run off when they needed her!

The little panda disappeared up the tree trunk and was soon invisible among the branches. Zoe sighed. Instead of finding one panda, now she'd lost two!

"Chi Chi!" she whispered again.

Suddenly there was a suspicious voice behind her. "Just what do you think you are doing, Miss Parker?"

Chapter Ten
Friends Forever

"Mr Pinch!" Zoe stammered, feeling her cheeks flush pink. Carefully she stepped to one side so that the zoo manager couldn't see the hole in the fence. "I was just...er ...looking for the pandas." She peered into the enclosure. "I thought I might be able to see them from this side of the enclosure, but I, um, can't."

The grumpy zoo manager glared at her. "Well, I'm looking for them myself," he told her bossily. "The crowd is fed up of waiting and I won't let those two little pests spoil the special event! They have to be around here somewhere." He peered into the enclosure and added crossly, "There are just so many of these big clumps of bamboo that they could have hidden behind!"

Zoe glanced up at the tree. Chi Chi's black and white face peered out from the branches. Then next to her there was a flash of black and white, and another face appeared. There wasn't just one baby panda in the tree, but two! Chi Chi had found Mei Mei!

Zoe had to hide her grin as Mr Pinch looked at her curiously.

There was another rustling sound
from inside the tree, and a high, happy
squeaking sound. Mr Pinch looked
around, puzzled. "Can you hear that?
There's definitely a panda close by!" he
muttered.

Zoe looked at Meep desperately. "We
can't let Mr Pinch see that the cubs are
out of their enclosure!" she whispered.
"Can you distract him?"

Meep's little face lit up. "I can be just as
cheeky as Chi Chi!" he told her proudly.

With a nimble leap he sprang over
to the zoo manager. It had rained that
morning and there was a muddy puddle
next to him. With a gleeful chirp, Meep
leaped into it, splashing mud on the zoo
manager's shiny shoes.

Mr Pinch stared down at the mess in

disbelief. "I polished my shoes this morning!" he spluttered. "You little nuisance! I'll have to clean these before the reporters see." He shook his head crossly and pointed a finger at Zoe. "If those pesky pandas haven't appeared by the time I back, I'm going into the enclosure and I'll search every inch until I find them!"

As Mr Pinch stomped off along the path, Zoe turned to the tree. "Chi Chi?" she called softly. "You can come down now. He's gone!"

There was a cheeky giggle, and Chi Chi slid down the tree trunk, her dark eyes bright. Then the branches shook gently again – and another face popped out of the leaves, squeaking happily.

"Mei Mei!" gasped Zoe, relief and happiness sweeping through her. "You were in the tree all along!"

"Hooray!" cried Meep, bouncing up and down.

Both pandas scrambled down from the tree. Zoe laughed as they leaped into her arms and they all shared a fluffy cuddle. "I'm so glad you're all right, Mei Mei," she told the little panda. "We were all so worried about you!

Chi Chi nuzzled Mei Mei with her black nose, squealing eagerly. "Mei Mei

was very brave to go exploring all by herself, Chi Chi," Zoe agreed, smiling. "And she *did* find the best hiding place yet from Mr Pinch! But I think you'd both better stay *inside* your home from now on, don't you?"

Mei Mei nodded, and Zoe grinned as the cubs squeaked and chattered in delight about their adventure. While they were apart, they had realised how much they missed one another, and now they were so happy to be back together, safe and sound.

Suddenly Meep tugged on Zoe's sleeve with his tiny fingers. "Quick, Zoe," he chirped. "Mr Pinch is back!"

Zoe placed the cubs carefully on the ground and they squeezed back through the hole in the fence and peeped out from behind the bamboo. The zoo manager was inside the enclosure, looking out at the grumbling crowd. "They must be in here somewhere," he announced, trying to sound cheerful.

"I've had enough of this," snapped one of the reporters. "I don't believe there really *are* any pandas in there. I think you've been making it all up!"

As Mr Pinch spluttered, Meep turned to Zoe. "If all those people leave without seeing the pandas, they'll be very cross," the little lemur chattered nervously. "They might even tell people not to come to the Rescue Zoo any more!"

"There's something even more important to think about, Meep," Zoe replied. "If Mr Pinch doesn't see that the pandas are getting along now, he might still decide to send one of them away. Remember, he said they had to be friends by today!"

She looked through the wire enclosure and laughed. "But I don't think we need to worry about that any more, Meep," she giggled happily. Side by side, Chi Chi and Mei Mei scampered out from behind the bamboo and padded towards the crowd. As they got closer, Mei Mei leaped playfully on to her sister and they rolled around in a pile of leaves, giggling and squealing. Chi Chi was proud of her brave sister. Even better, Mei Mei was no longer too timid and frightened to try new things. In fact, Mei Mei seemed just as bold and brave as Chi Chi – rolling, scampering and having fun in her home more than ever before.

"After their big adventure, the cubs
have realised how much they love each
other!" Zoe grinned as she listened to
their excited squeals. "They've made
friends for good this time."

Suddenly the reporters spotted them, and there were gasps and laughs from the crowd. "Look – there they are!" one cried. "I don't believe it. They're even cuter than I imagined!"

"And look at them playing together. They're gorgeous," added another, taking a picture.

Mr Pinch stared at the pandas, completely baffled. "Where on earth were the little fluffballs hiding?" he muttered. "I looked *everywhere*!"

While the crowd were busy watching the pandas, Zoe covered up the hole in the fence with an armful of dry sticks and twigs. "We'll make sure Stephanie fixes it properly later," she whispered to Meep. "But something tells me the cubs won't be trying to escape again any time soon!"

Quietly they slipped back to the gate and out on to the path. Zoe ran up behind Stephanie and Great-Uncle Horace, and tapped them both on the shoulder.

"There you are, sweetheart!" Stephanie cried, throwing her arms around Zoe.

"I was wondering where you were. Quick, take a look at Chi Chi and Mei Mei! I don't know what's happened, but suddenly they're getting along so well!"

"It's extraordinary," added Great-Uncle Horace, his brown eyes twinkling at Zoe. "And just in time!"

The gate opened again and out came Mr Pinch. Zoe waited for him to storm and shout about the naughty cubs but the zoo manager was delighted. "The reporters say they'll tell all their friends to come to the zoo to see the pandas," he announced smugly. "One of them even promised to write a special story about how rare they are. You don't see twin pandas every day, after all. That means extra visitors for the Rescue Zoo – and extra money! It was a brilliant idea of

mine, making sure we kept them both."
He strolled off down the path, whistling
a happy tune.

"Will the sisters always be together, Mr
Higgins?" called a reporter, holding a
microphone out to Great-Uncle Horace.

"Always," he replied, beaming at Zoe.
"The cubs are not just sisters. They are
also the very best of friends. We would
never dream of separating them."

Zoe beamed back at Great-Uncle Horace and turned to watch the baby pandas rolling around together. She was so relieved, and so happy! The twins were both going to stay at the Rescue Zoo and enjoy being together.

Just then Mei Mei leaped into the waterfall, splashing Chi Chi.

The crowd chuckled and Meep giggled so hard he fell over! Zoe grinned and scooped her little friend into her arms for a hug. "It looks like the Rescue Zoo doesn't have just one playful panda any more, Meep," she whispered happily. "Now we have two!"

Look out for more amazing animal adventures at the Rescue Zoo!

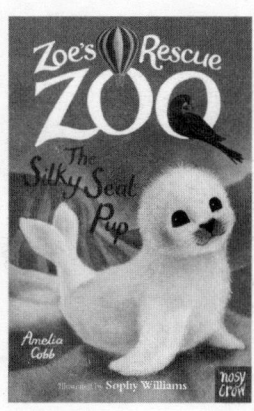

The Rescue Princesses

Have you read?

Look out for: